NANCY DREW
AND THE CLUE CREW

#24

Princess Mix-up Mystery

BY CAROLYN KEENE

ILLUSTRATED BY MACKY PAMINTUAN

Aladdin
New York London Toronto Sydney

❦ ALADDIN

An imprint of Simon & Schuster Children's Publishing Division
1230 Avenue of the Americas, New York, NY 10020
First Aladdin paperback edition January 2010
Text copyright © 2010 by Simon & Schuster, Inc.
Illustrations copyright © 2010 by Macky Pamintuan
All rights reserved, including the right of reproduction in whole or in part in any form.
ALADDIN is a trademark of Simon & Schuster, Inc., and related logo is a registered trademark of Simon & Schuster, Inc.
NANCY DREW, NANCY DREW AND THE CLUE CREW, and related logos are registered trademarks of Simon & Schuster, Inc.
For information about special discounts for bulk purchases, please contact Simon & Schuster Special Sales at 1-866-506-1949 or business@simonandschuster.com.
The Simon & Schuster Speakers Bureau can bring authors to your live event. For more information or to book an event contact the Simon & Schuster Speakers Bureau at 1-866-248-3049 or visit our website at www.simonspeakers.com.
Designed by Lisa Vega
The text of this book was set in ITC Stone Informal.
Manufactured in the United States of America
10 9 8 7 6 5 4 3
Library of Congress Control Number 2009924063
ISBN 978-1-4169-7811-4
ISBN 978-1-4169-9855-6 (eBook)
0710 OFF

CONTENTS

CHAPTER ONE

Once Upon a Guess

"Can't we run errands later, Nancy?" Bess Marvin asked, pointing to her daisy-shaped watch. "We'll miss the opening of Prissy's Princess Parlor!"

"Prissy is a good name for that place," George Fayne scoffed. "Who else but prissy girly-girls would go there?"

Eight-year-old Nancy Drew smiled at her two best friends as they walked side by side down River Street. "Prissy is short for Priscilla, George," she explained. "She and her sister, Wendy, own the Princess Parlor!"

"Where else can girls like us can get our hair styled and topped off with a princess-pretty tiara?" Bess asked. "It's a dream come true!"

"You mean a *nightmare*," George groaned. "I'll bet even the computers in that place are pink."

"Is that all you can think about?" Bess asked. "Computers?"

"When I'm not thinking about printers, scanners, and speakers!" George answered with a grin.

Bess rolled her eyes. "Are you sure you're my cousin?" She sighed.

"Come on, you guys," Nancy said, picking up her pace. "Errands first, fun later."

River Street was the busiest street in River Heights. Besides the usual stores Nancy saw tiny green buds on the trees that lined the street. Not only was it spring break, it was the first week of spring—and spring was Nancy's favorite season!

"First stop," Nancy said as they turned toward a store in the middle of the block, The Mean Bean Health Store.

Nancy, Bess, and George filed through the door of the Mean Bean. There to greet them was Kevin Garcia. Kevin was in the girls' third grade class at River Heights Elementary School. Kevin's parents owned the Mean Bean, but he acted like he owned it himself.

"Welcome to the Mean Bean, Clue Crew!" Kevin declared.

Nancy smiled at the mention of their detective club, the Clue Crew. Everyone at school knew that she, Bess, and George loved solving mysteries. And were good at it too!

"What do you need?" Kevin asked, rubbing his hands together. "If it's all-natural, we've got it."

"Hannah needs something stinky that will keep deer from nibbling her flower garden," Nancy explained.

"How about George's sneakers?" Bess joked.

"Ha, ha," George said, not really laughing.

Hannah Gruen had been the Drews' housekeeper since Nancy was three years old. Not only was Hannah as sweet as her cupcakes— she was the next best thing to a mom!

3

"Do you have the deer repellent?" Nancy asked.

"I told you, we have everything!" Kevin boomed. "Um . . . everything except natural stinky deer repellent."

Nancy frowned. She didn't want to disappoint Hannah, but the Mean Bean was the only natural store in town.

"It's okay, Nancy, we'll find something else," Bess said. "Now we can go to Prissy's Princess Parlor!"

Kevin raced to the door as the girls left the store. "Did you say parlor?" he shouted after them. "We sell all-natural shampoo here! Organic nail polish! Even lipstick made out of pulverized soybeans!"

Kevin's voice trailed off as the girls headed down River Street.

"Hannah will be so disappointed." Nancy sighed.

"But the deer—cartwheels!" George said, as they walked along.

Prissy's Princess Parlor wasn't hard to find. It

was the only store with a door decorated with purple and gold balloons. It was also the only store surrounded by reporters, photographers, and cheering girls.

"Now," Mayor Strong said, holding a pair of scissors. "Prissy's Princess Parlor shall live happily ever after!"

Prissy and Wendy Darling held opposite ends of a ribbon stretched in front of the door. Nancy noticed that the door was painted like a castle gate.

"It's just like a fairy tale," Nancy breathed as the mayor ceremoniously snipped the ribbon in half.

"If this is a fairy tale," George said, "there's the ogre!"

"Ogre?" Nancy asked. She looked up to see where George was pointing. Standing at the window above the store was an angry-looking man. His mouth was a grim line as he scowled down at the cheering crowd.

"That's Marvin Dretzel the Human Pretzel,"

Bess explained. "He owns the Yay for Yoga studio upstairs."

"How do you know?" George asked.

"My mom takes a class there," Bess said. "She says yoga helps her to relax."

Nancy watched as Marvin slammed down

the window with a bang. He didn't look very relaxed to her!

"Okay, princesses," Prissy shouted to the crowd. "Are you in it to win it?"

More cheers, as both sisters undraped a thick white mattress on the sidewalk.

"The princess who guesses how many peas are under this mattress wins a free salon treatment tomorrow for her and two of her BFFs!" Wendy shouted. "And their picture in the paper."

Nancy was superexcited now. The contest was just like her favorite fairy tale, "The Princess and the Pea."

"Let's all try to guess," Bess said.

"No way!" George cried. "Even if I won, I wouldn't go in that princess parlor. Besides, I can't go tomorrow."

"Why not?" Bess asked.

"Trina Vanderhoof asked me to join her girls' basketball team, the Blue Jets," George answered. She pretended to dribble a make-believe ball. "The first game is tomorrow."

7

"But you could be a princess!" Bess exclaimed.

"Princess, schmincess." George rolled her eyes. "Who needs a royal court when you can be on a basketball court?"

"Okay, okay," Nancy said, tugging George's arm. "But stand in line with us for good luck."

Nancy, Bess, and George hurried to the back of the line. A girl wearing a pink tiara was about to climb on the mattress when two bigger girls pushed in front of her.

One began measuring the mattress with a measuring tape. The other listened to it with a doctor's stethoscope!

"Don't those two go to our school?" Bess asked.

Nancy nodded and said, "It's Suki Sussman and Ella Knox. They belong to the Rad Scientists Club."

"That explains it," George said. "They're probably trying to figure out scientifically how many peas are under the mattress."

Suki and Ella worked until Mayor Strong stepped in. "Girls, even princesses have to wait their turn," he said.

"Yeah!" The tiara girl sneered. "Take a royal hike!"

Suki and Ella grumbled as they trudged to the back of the line. But the moment they saw Nancy, Bess, and George their jaws dropped.

"We were standing where you are!" Suki complained. "You took our place!"

"We didn't see you when we got here," Nancy said.

Nancy could hear Suki and Ella grumbling as they slipped behind her and her friends. She tried to ignore the Rad Scientists as she turned back to the contest. Every girl so far had guessed the wrong number of peas.

Finally it was Bess's turn. She hopped on the mattress and lay on her back.

"Thirty peas," Bess guessed out loud. "That's my lucky number times ten."

"A good guess, but wrong," Mayor Strong said.

"Phooey," Bess said, hopping off the mattress. "Time to get a new lucky number."

Next was Nancy's turn. She climbed on the mattress, laid back, and stared at sky as she took a guess.

"Is it one pea?" Nancy asked. "That's how many peas were under the mattress in 'The Princess and the Pea.'"

"But not under this mattress," Mayor Strong replied.

Nancy's heart sank as she scooted off the mattress to join her friends. She and Bess had no chance of winning the princess makeover now. Unless . . .

"Take a guess, George," Nancy said. "If you win you can pick us to go with you."

"I told you, Nancy," George said, shaking her head. "You can't pay me to enter that prissy princess contest!"

"Looks like someone already did," Bess said. She pointed to a bill crumpled on the middle of the mattress.

"That's the ten dollar bill Hannah gave me for the deer repellent," Nancy gasped. "It must have fallen out of my pocket while I was guessing."

"Got it," George said. She crawled across the mattress. She was about to grab the bill when Mayor Strong shouted out: "Next princess—take a guess!"

"Huh?" George gulped. "No, I just wanted to—"

"Guess, guess!" the crowd chanted.

George rolled her eyes and flopped on her back.

"Okay. I guess fifty-five," George said. "That's how many are in a frozen bag of peas. I helped my mom count some for one of her catering jobs. Can I get off now?"

Mayor Strong blasted the trumpet so loud it

made George bounce. Photographers snapped George's picture as she sat up, stunned.

"Girls—we have a winner!" Mayor Strong shouted. "Long live Princess Georgia!"

CHAPTER TWO

Thrones and Groans

"Did he say princess?" Nancy gasped.

"Princess Georgia! Princess Georgia!" the crowd chanted. "Long live Princess Georgia!"

George leaped off the mattress shouting, "My name's George! Nobody but my grandmother calls me Georgia!"

Nancy and Bess cheered too. They knew George hated her real name, but she *had* just won a free makeover at Prissy's Princess Parlor for herself and her friends. And those friends would surely be them!

A photographer from the River Heights *Daily News* snapped George's picture.

"Way to go, George!" Nancy cheered as she

and Bess ran to join their friend. Suki and Ella ran over too, but not to congratulate George.

"Fifty-five peas was *my* answer," Suki complained. "If you guys hadn't jumped in front of us, I would have won!"

"You can have the prize," George said. "I have to play basketball tomorrow."

"George, are you serious?" Nancy cried. "If you go to the princess parlor you get to pick two friends!"

"Sorry," George sighed. "But I don't want—"

"You owe me a favor, George Fayne!" Bess cut in.

"What favor?" George asked slowly.

"May I remind you that I secretly ate your string beans at Grandma's house last Thanksgiving?" Bess asked.

George gritted her teeth. Nancy knew she hated string beans even more than girly-girl makeovers.

"Well?" Bess asked, raising an eyebrow.

"Okay, you win," George said. "But Trina is

going to flip when I can't play tomorrow."

"Play basketball *after* your makeover," Nancy said.

"With pink nails and glitter in my hair?" George exclaimed. "I don't think so!"

Just then, George was whisked aside by Prissy and Wendy, who smiled as they presented her with the winning certificate.

"Princess George?" a reporter from the *Daily News* asked. "Who will be joining you for your royal makeover?"

"Nancy Drew and Bess Marvin," George replied. "I guess you could say I couldn't have won without them."

All three friends smiled for the photographer until a scowling Marvin Dretzel pushed past the girls.

"I'm not here to judge, Mister Mayor, but the noise is unacceptable!" Marvin declared. "How can my students find inner peace with a gaggle of girls downstairs every day?"

"Don't get your joints in a twist, Marv," Mayor

Strong said. "Little princesses never make a lot of noise."

"Princess power! Princess power! Princess power!" the girls in the crowd shouted.

"Well," Marvin huffed. "I certainly hope this place doesn't last too long."

"What a grump," Nancy said as Marvin stomped back to his upstairs studio. But as she gazed into the crowd she spotted two more grumpy faces—those of Suki and Ella.

Looks like those Rad Scientists, Nancy thought, *are mad scientists!*

"What if I don't recognize you later?" Hannah asked the next morning.

"Just look for three princesses!" Nancy suggested.

It was Wednesday morning and the three girls had a plan. Hannah would leave Nancy, Bess, and George at Prissy's Princess Parlor and pick them up after their makeovers.

"Did you ever find that all-natural deer repellent, Hannah?" Bess asked as they approached the salon.

"Not yet, I'm afraid," Hannah sighed. "And my tulips will bud any day now."

Hannah opened the door of Prissy's Princess Parlor. A tiny fairy bell jingled as Hannah and the girls filed into the salon.

"Welcome, fair princesses!" Prissy said, taking a deep bow. "I am your lady-in-waiting Priscilla!"

"Wow!" Nancy said as they looked around.

The walls of the parlor were painted deep rosy-pink. Purple velvet chairs faced mirrors surrounded by gold frames. Hanging from the ceiling were crystal wind chimes and tiny porcelain fairies.

"It's magical!" Bess gasped.

The girls hung up their jackets. After Hannah said good-bye and left the parlor, Prissy turned to the girls and smiled.

"You'll be happy to know that two other princesses are holding court today," Prissy informed them.

"Really? Who?" Nancy asked.

ZIIIIIIP! Prissy pulled open a velvet curtain. Behind it were Suki and Ella, getting their nails polished by Wendy.

"Surprise!" Suki sneered. "We wanted to see what we could have won if you hadn't jumped in front of us."

"Too bad our allowances only pay for manicures," Ella complained, holding up rainbow-colored nails.

Nancy rolled her eyes at Bess and George.

Suki and Ella were still mad. And they wouldn't let them forget it!

"Time to let your nails dry, princesses Suki and Ella," Wendy declared in a chirpy voice. "In the meantime let's get our three new princesses into their royal robes."

"As if *we* ever got royal robes," Ella grumbled.

The sisters led Nancy, Bess, and George into the back room. Hanging on a rack were red cloth beauty capes.

"Hurry and change," Wendy said excitedly. "You must turn into princesses before the clock strikes twelve, just like Cinderella."

The girls glanced at the clock. Eleven fifty-three. Only seven minutes to change!

The girls raced to the rack. They each took a robe and slipped it over their heads. Bess's arms got stuck in the sleeves but after a lot of wiggling they popped out.

"We did it," George pointed to the clock. "In five minutes flat!"

"Well done, princesses," Prissy exclaimed.

"Now if you'll please follow me—your royal makeovers await!"

"Still wish you were playing basketball?" Nancy whispered to George as they followed the sisters.

"Nah," George whispered. "Just don't tell Trina I'm having fun."

The girls stepped from the back room into the parlor. The velvet curtain was still pulled back. But Suki and Ella were no longer behind it.

"Where'd they go?" Wendy wondered.

"Their jackets are gone," Prissy said, nodding at the coat rack. "They must have left."

"Their nails can't be dry yet." Wendy sighed. "They'll spoil their manicures for sure."

"Better than spoiling our fun!" Bess whispered.

"M'ladies," Prissy said, waving her hand toward three purple velvet salon chairs. "Your thrones await!"

Nancy, Bess, and George each sat down in a velvet chair. They gazed at their reflections in the mirrors as Prissy and Wendy got to work.

After much brushing and styling the girls were princess-perfect. Bess's long blond ponytail was curled and tied with a blue velvet ribbon. Nancy's reddish-blond hair was swept high on her head and fastened with a bejeweled clip. George's dark curls were pinned with barrettes shaped like baseball bats.

"Cool!" George said, admiring her reflection.

"Hannah was right!" Nancy said, patting the back of her hairdo. "She won't recognize us!"

"And this is just the beginning," Wendy said. "There are still manicures and a bit of face painting to come."

"But before you get up from your thrones," Prissy said, holding up a pink spray-pump bottle, "the finishing touch."

"What is it?" Nancy asked.

"A lovely finishing spray called Strawberry Spritz," Prissy explained, waving the pink bottle. "It'll leave your hair smelling like fresh strawberries."

"And it's all natural!" Wendy added.

Prissy stepped back. She then sprayed each girl's hairdo one by one. Nancy took a whiff and began to gag. The Strawberry Spritz didn't smell like strawberries at all.

It smelled like *rotten eggs*!

"The stuff reeks!" Nancy said, squeezing her nose.

"And look at our hair!" Bess cried, pointing to the mirror. "It's turning *blue*!"

CHAPTER THREE

Hairy Scary

"My hair is strawberry blond—not *blueberry* blond!" Nancy gasped.

"I-I-I don't know how that happened!" Prissy stammered, staring at the bottle. "This is supposed to smell like strawberries—not rotten eggs!"

"As for the blue, we don't have a clue!" Wendy said.

Prissy ran to the shelf that held more bottles of Strawberry Spritz. She uncapped each of the other bottles and took a whiff. "These all smell like strawberry," she said. "I don't understand. . . ."

Nancy, Bess, and George were out of their

chairs, staring at their reflections in the mirror.

"We can't let anyone see us like this!" Bess cried.

Nancy totally agreed. Until—

"Greetings, fair princesses!" a man's voice boomed.

The girls whirled around. Walking into the Princess Parlor was Mayor Strong. Right behind him were the photographer and reporter from the River Heights *Daily News*!

"Say cheese!" Mayor Strong declared.

Before the girls could cover their heads, the photographer snapped their picture. But when the mayor noticed their blue hair, he gasped.

"Blue hair?" the reporter tilted her head as she studied the girls. "Is this the cool new look for girls?"

"No!" Nancy, Bess, and George said at the same time.

"What's that smell?" the photographer asked.

"We had a bit of a glitch this morning," Prissy explained as she hurried the visitors toward the door. "You'll have to leave while we wash the girls' hair."

Nancy, Bess, and George exchanged glum looks. Even the shoulders of their royal robes were stained blue!

"What's making our hair so stinky?" Bess asked.

"It's the smell of something fishy," Nancy answered.

"Not fish, Nancy," George said. "Rotten eggs!"

Nancy shook her head and whispered, "I mean someone messed up that Strawberry Spritz bottle on purpose."

"Who?" Bess whispered.

"That's what the Clue Crew is going to find out," Nancy said. "But first we have to put our heads together."

While Prissy and Wendy gathered fresh towels and shampoo, Nancy spotted Kevin Garcia outside the window.

"Why is Kevin peeking in here?" Nancy said.

"No boys allowed!" Bess shouted to the window.

Kevin must have heard Bess because he turned from the window and ran away.

"Did you see that look on Kevin's face?" George asked. "Are we that scary?"

The girls glanced back at the mirror and answered at the same time: "YES!"

❀ ❀ ❀

"Should I wash my hair one more time, Hannah?" Nancy asked the next morning.

"You had your hair washed well at the parlor yesterday," Hannah said as she blow-dried Nancy's damp hair. "I'm sure the stuff is out by now."

"I want to be extra-sure," Nancy said. "My own dog won't even come near me!"

Nancy's Labrador puppy, Chocolate Chip, lay on the floor right outside the bathroom door. Chip whined as she covered her nose with her paws.

"All dry," Hannah said. She switched off the noisy hairdryer just in time for Nancy to hear the doorbell.

"That's probably Bess and George," Nancy said, tossing her freshly washed hair. She ran down the stairs and opened the door.

There stood Bess and George, both with wet hair.

"We washed our hair a hundred times to get the blue out," George explained.

"I even sprayed on my mom's perfume to cover up the eggy smell," Bess said. "It's called Eau de Paris."

"More like Eau de P. U.!" George said, fanning the air with her hand.

Nancy invited Bess and George into the house. Her father was finishing breakfast before going to his job at the law firm.

"Did you see the morning paper, girls?" Mr. Drew asked. The River Heights *Daily News* was on the table next to his place mat.

"Why? Are the comics really funny today, Mr. Drew?" Bess asked.

"The comics might be," Mr. Drew said. He held up the paper and sighed. "But this isn't."

Nancy and her friends gasped at the front page. Splashed on it was a picture of them at Prissy's Princess Parlor—blue hair and all!

"It's us," Nancy gasped.

"That's the picture they took at the Princess Parlor!" George groaned.

Nancy couldn't believe her eyes. The front

page was usually black and white. Today it was in color—so everyone could see their blue hair!

"Princess Parlor Closes After Royal Blunder." Nancy read the headline out loud.

"Well, that's good news, isn't it?" Mr. Drew asked. "Now it won't happen to any other girls."

Nancy shook her head. It wasn't good news at all.

"The makeover mess wasn't Prissy's or Wendy's fault, Daddy," Nancy explained. "We're going to find out who did this so they can open the parlor again."

"The way it's supposed to be!" Bess added.

"If anyone can do it," Mr. Drew said as he folded the paper, "it's the Clue Crew!"

"Thanks, Mr. Drew," George said. "And we already have a pretty good idea who did it."

"We do? Who?" Bess asked as they left the kitchen.

"Duh!" George groaned. "Suki and Ella were mad at us for winning the contest, remember?"

"Suki and Ella were at the parlor yesterday too," Nancy added. "They could have messed with the bottle of Strawberry Spritz while we were in the back room."

"Why didn't I think of that?" Bess asked.

"Because you washed your hair ten times last night, Bess," George said. "Your brain is probably waterlogged!"

Nancy buttoned up her spring jacket with the deep pockets. They were already stuffed with clear plastic bags for collecting clues.

"Suki and Ella are our biggest suspects," Nancy said. "But we need to find clues at Prissy's Princess Parlor before we accuse them of anything."

"If it's still open." Bess sighed.

The girls all had the same rule—they could walk anywhere as long as it wasn't more than five blocks from their houses—and as long as they were together.

Nancy blew good-bye kisses to her father and Hannah. Then she and her friends left the house for River Street.

"Do you think we'll solve this case before spring break ends?" Bess asked.

"I hope so," Nancy admitted. "I would hate to go back to school not knowing who our enemies are."

"Speaking of enemies," George whispered. "Here comes one of mine."

Nancy turned to see Trina walking toward them.

"Hey, George!" Trina shouted meanly. "Thanks for making sure we lost yesterday." She glared at George. "We lost by two points!" She held up two fingers. "Two stupid little points!"

Nancy stared at Trina's fingers as she waved them in front of their faces.

"You had to go to that dumb Princess Parlor," Trina said. "Since when do you like places like that, George?"

"George won us free makeovers," Bess explained. "Hair styles, manicures, pedicures—"

"Yeah, yeah, I heard all about those makeovers!" Trina cut in with a laugh. "I guess the Clue Crew turned into the *Blue* Crew!"

Trina stormed past the girls and up the block. "Blue Crew," George scoffed. "That's so funny I forgot to laugh."

"Trina shouldn't talk," Nancy said.

"What do you mean?" Bess asked.

Nancy turned to her friends, her eyes flashing. "Didn't you notice something about Trina's fingers?" she asked.

"She held up two," George said. "So what?"

"Two," Nancy said with a smile. "And *blue*!"

32

CHAPTER FOUR

Caught Blue-Handed

"Maybe Trina got blue fingers when she poured the stinky stuff in the bottle," Nancy explained.

"Trina would have washed her hands since yesterday, don't you think?" Bess asked.

"Not really," Nancy said. "Trina is so sporty she makes George look like a flower fairy!"

"Very funny," George said, hands on her hips.

"Trina was supermad at George for not playing basketball," Nancy went on. "Maybe she was mad enough to get even."

"But how?" George asked. "Trina wasn't even *at* the Princess Parlor yesterday."

"And she never will be!" Bess said, her eyes

wide. "You heard her say how much she hates the place."

"Then how do you explain the blue-stained fingers?" Nancy asked, tapping her chin as she thought.

"Maybe Trina was eating a blue Popsicle," Bess said cheerily.

"Maybe," Nancy said. "But I still think the blue is a clue!"

It was still early as they walked, but River Street was busy with shoppers and kids having fun on their last days of spring break.

"You guys," George suggested as they neared the parlor, "let's not tell Prissy and Wendy we want to look for clues."

"Why not?" Nancy asked.

"Some grown-ups don't get kids being detectives," George answered. She rolled her eyes. "They think we're just *playing*!"

"Got it," Nancy agreed.

When the girls reached the Princess Parlor, Prissy and Wendy were outside. One sister was sadly taking down the balloons. The other was taping a sign on the door that read: CLOSED.

"They can't close the store without us looking for clues!" Nancy whispered.

"I have an idea," Bess whispered back. She ran toward the sisters shouting, "Wait! Don't close the store yet!"

"Why not?" Prissy asked.

"I think I dropped my earring when I was getting my hair styled yesterday," Bess blurted.

"Oh, dear!" Wendy said. "What did it look like?"

"Like this," Bess said. She tugged at the little beaded earring hanging from her earlobe. "Did you see it?"

"Um . . . yeah," Wendy said, cocking her head. "It's right there on your other earlobe."

Bess's eyes widened. She then blurted, "That's the third one and a spare! In case I lose one. Which I already did, so . . ."

"Go ahead," Prissy said. She unlocked the door and opened it for the girls.

The Clue Crew went straight to the purple velvet chairs they sat in yesterday. Nancy found a wastebasket under the counter and peeked inside. The first thing she saw was a pink spray-pump bottle.

"That's got to be the bottle Prissy used on us," Nancy whispered.

George lifted it from the wastebasket. She took a whiff of the nozzle and said, "Ew! It's the one, all right!"

Nancy took the bottle from George. She turned it around in her hand looking for clues.

"No fingerprints," Nancy said. "Just a stinky bottle."

She was about to toss the bottle into the wastebasket when she noticed something stuck on the bottom of the bottle. It was a price label with a blue smudge!

"Look!" Nancy said as she pointed out the smudge. "Whoever poured the stinky stuff inside must have gotten some on the label."

"Or," Bess said. "Suki and Ella had their nails painted lots of colors. If their nails were still wet one of them could have gotten blue nail polish on the label."

"Whatever it is," Nancy said, carefully peeling off the label and dropping it into a clue bag, "it's a clue.

"Done!" she said, sliding the bag back into her pocket. "Let's go now, so Prissy and Wendy can close up."

The girls walked to the door. They were about to say good-bye when Wendy held out what looked like a folded note.

"Can you do us a favor, pretty please?" Wendy asked. "Can you go upstairs and give this note to Marvin Dretzel?"

"Dretzel the human pretzel?" George asked.

"It's a good-bye note," Prissy explained. "We're not sure if he knows we're leaving today."

Nancy shuddered as she remembered Marvin's grumpy face. But she forced a smile and said, "Sure, we'll do it."

"You're so neat!" Wendy said, handing the note to Nancy. She turned to Bess and asked, "Did you find what you were looking for?"

"We sure did!" Bess said, eyeing Nancy's pocket.

The girls entered the doorway that led to the Yay for Yoga studio.

"Why would Prissy and Wendy want to say good-bye to someone who doesn't want them here?" Nancy wondered as they climbed the staircase.

"Maybe it doesn't say good-bye," George chuckled. "Maybe it says 'so long, sucker!'"

At the top of the stairs the girls found the Yay for Yoga door. A sign on it read, CLASS IN SESSION.

"I'll slide it under the door," Nancy decided.

But as she crouched down she caught a whiff of something sweet.

"Bess! George!" Nancy said. "Do you smell that?"

Bess and George wiggled their noses as they sniffed the air too.

"Strawberries," Bess said. "It's coming from inside the studio."

"Do you think Marvin emptied out the bottle of Strawberry Spritz," Nancy whispered, "and filled it with the stinky blue stuff right here in his studio?"

"That's pretty twisted," George said, shaking her head. "Even for a human pretzel!"

"Don't you remember how much he hated the noise outside the other day?" Nancy asked.

"He also said he hoped Prissy's Princess Parlor wouldn't last long!" Bess gasped. "I heard it with my own ears."

The girls gasped as the door was flung open. Staring down at them was Marvin Dretzel!

"H-h-hi," Nancy stammered. "We were just—"

39

"I'm not here to judge," Marvin said, quickly opening the door wider. "But you girls are late for class."

Nancy looked past Marvin into the studio. Several kids were sitting cross-legged on the floor.

"Get into the lotus position right away so we can meditate," Marvin said, ushering the girls into the studio.

"What did he say?" George said.

"He means twist ourselves up like pretzels and daydream," Bess whispered. "That's what my mom does."

"Let's do it," Nancy whispered. "Maybe we can find out where that strawberry smell is coming from."

Nancy stuffed Wendy's note in her pocket as they followed Marvin into the studio. It was a big room with a desk against one wall and a metal shelf against another. The brick walls were covered with feel-good posters that said stuff like: "When Life Throws You Lemons, Make Lemonade," and "Don't Let the Turkeys Get You Down."

Copying the others the girls sat cross-legged on the floor. Marvin sat the same way as he called out in a soft voice, "Close your eyes and let your thoughts float like a Frisbee. Let them whiz by over your head . . . whiz by . . ."

"You don't let it whiz by, you catch it," George whispered. "Didn't he ever play Frisbee?"

"He's trying to make us relax," Bess whispered.

"Shhhh!" the other kids warned.

Everyone's eyes were closed except the Clue Crew's. Theirs darted around the room looking for clues.

"Look!" George suddenly whispered.

Nancy turned to see George pointing to the shelf. On it were books, DVDs, a plant, and four familiar-looking bottles. Bess let out a little gasp when she saw them too.

"Omigosh," Bess whispered. "Those bottles look just like Strawberry Spritz!"

Nancy agreed. No wonder the place smelled like strawberries. "Come on. Let's check it out!" she whispered.

The girls were about to stand when one of Marvin's eyes blinked open. They froze back into position. But when Marvin closed his eyes again Nancy stood up. So did George.

Both girls tiptoed to the shelf. Nancy picked up a bottle then gave George a thumbs-up.

"Strawberry Spritz!" Nancy whispered.

"Sweet!" George whispered back. "Where's Bess?"

Bess? Nancy turned to see Bess still sitting cross-legged on the floor.

"Nancy, George, help!" Bess hissed. "My legs—they're stuck!"

CHAPTER FIVE

Strawberry Spritz Forever

"Great," George groaned as she and Nancy ran over to help Bess. The other kids opened their eyes to see what all the commotion was about.

"Hi, guys!" Shelby Metcalf said cheerily. "You didn't tell me you joined this class too."

"We didn't," Bess said as her legs finally popped apart. "We're here to solve to a mystery—"

George clapped her hand over Bess's mouth. But it was too late.

"Mystery?" a boy wearing a blue sweat suit asked. "You mean you're spies?"

"Bad karma," said a girl dressed in a tie-dyed T-shirt and leggings.

"It certainly is!" Marvin said as he squeezed

through the small crowd of kids. "I don't under-stand why you girls have to play detective in my yoga class."

"We're not playing!" Bess said in a muffled voice behind George's hand. She pulled the hand off and added, "Why are all these kids here anyway? We thought you hated kids—"

Nancy clapped her hand over Bess's mouth this time.

"Mmmph!" Bess protested.

"It's just that you didn't look too happy when Prissy's Princess Parlor opened downstairs, Mr. Dretzel," Nancy explained.

"That's true," Marvin admitted. "I thought all that noise would interrupt our peace and serenity."

"Just as we thought." Nancy sighed, letting go of Bess's mouth.

"But that same day," Marvin went on. "I got this fabulous idea for a brand-new class—a yoga class for children called Kids for Karma."

"What *is* karma?" Nancy asked.

"Karma is what we create with our thoughts and actions," Marvin explained.

"Okay," George said slowly. "So did your karma create the shutting down of Prissy's Princess Parlor?"

"Of course not!" Marvin declared. He raised an eyebrow as he studied the girls. "Hey . . . aren't you those little princesses who turned blue?"

"That's us," Nancy said, feeling her cheeks redden. "Someone switched the Strawberry Spritz in the bottle with some stinky blue stuff."

"Well, it certainly wasn't me!" Marvin said defensively.

"Then what's with all those bottles of Strawberry Spritz on your shelf?" George asked.

"The Strawberry Spritz is used strictly for aromatherapy," Marvin explained. "My students relax better when the air smells nice."

"You mean like strawberries?" Bess asked.

"Ahhh, yes," Marvin said, shutting his eyes. "We simply imagine that we're floating peacefully down a thick strawberry milkshake river!"

"Can we float down a chocolate milkshake instead?" a boy with freckles asked.

"Pistachio!" a girl shouted.

"Butter pecan!" another girl exclaimed.

Marvin rolled his eyes and muttered, "Kids."

While the kids shouted out their favorite flavors, the Clue Crew stepped to the side.

"How do we know he's telling the truth?" George asked.

Nancy didn't know until she remembered the sisters' note in her pocket. She pulled it out and said, "Maybe this has a clue."

Bess and George peered over Nancy's shoulder as she softly read the note aloud: "'Dear Marvin, It was so nice being your downstairs neighbor. We hope you enjoy the four bottles of Strawberry Spritz you bought from us yesterday. Prissy and Wendy.'"

"No clue there," George said. "We know he must have gotten the bottles from the salon."

Nancy turned to the shelf and counted the bottles. One . . . two . . . three . . . four.

"Marvin is innocent," Nancy declared.

"How do you know?" Bess asked.

"Do the math," Nancy said. "Marvin bought four bottles. And four bottles are still on the shelf."

"Oh!" Bess said, her eyes lighting up. "So Marvin couldn't have filled one of the bottles with the stinky blue stuff and put it downstairs—"

"Because all four bottles are right there!" George finished, nodding at the shelf. "Good catch, Nancy!"

The girls turned back to the kids. This time

they were each standing on one foot.

"Come on, girls," Marvin called. "We're in the flamingo position now."

"We have to go now, Mr. Dretzel," Nancy said politely.

As the girls left the studio, they found Shelby right behind them.

"I'm over that class too," Shelby said as they headed downstairs. "I'd rather eat a pretzel than be one."

Once outside, Shelby pointed to the closed salon. "Bummer what happened to you in there," she said. "I wonder if the same thing happened to Trina."

"You mean Trina Vanderhoof?" Nancy asked.

Shelby nodded and said, "I saw Trina coming out of the parlor yesterday morning. She walked fast and looked around as if she didn't want anyone to see her."

The girls traded surprised looks. They thought Trina would never, ever go into Prissy's Princess Parlor.

"Are you sure it was Trina?" George asked.

"Sure I'm sure," Shelby said. "When I said hi she came over to me and looked me straight in the eye."

"What did she say?" Bess asked.

"She said, 'You didn't see me coming out of this place, okay?'" Shelby repeated in a gruff voice. "I guess she didn't want me to tell anybody."

"You just did," Bess said.

"Oops!" Shelby gasped. She gave a little wave before running up the block and around the corner.

"She goofed." George sighed.

"No, she didn't!" Nancy said excitedly. "Shelby gave us a great clue—she told us Trina *was* at Prissy's Princess Parlor yesterday!"

"And if Trina's fingers were blue," Bess said, "the smudge on the label could have come from her!"

"Let's see if there's a clue in the blue," Nancy said as she pulled out the clue bag and the label.

"Wait a minute," Bess said. She dug into her own pocket and pulled out glasses with funny-looking lenses. "Let me look at it through these."

"What is that?" George cried.

"Another gizmo I built myself," Bess said, blinking behind the glasses. "I call it the 'I-Spy Magnifying Specs.'"

Nancy giggled. Bess was great at building and fixing things. But the magnifying specs made her eyes look tremendous—like a bug's!

"What do you see, Bess?" Nancy asked.

After a few more seconds of peering through the glasses Bess gave a little gasp. "I spy a fingerprint," she said excitedly. "And a great clue!"

Chapter Six

Sticky Situation

The Clue Crew had a new plan. They would compare Trina's fingerprint with the one Bess found on the label. But first they needed Trina's fingerprints.

"Are you sure this is going to work?" Bess asked later that afternoon.

George twirled a basketball on her finger as they walked through the park. Nancy held a bottle of craft glue in her hand.

"Sure I'm sure," George said. "All we do is smear my old basketball with glue. Then I pass the ball to Trina and if we're lucky, she passes it back."

"Then we peel off the glue and ta-daaa!"

Nancy explained. "Trina's fingerprints will be all over it!"

"The trick is straight from the Junior Sleuth website," George explained. "So it's got to work!"

Nancy, Bess, and George could see Trina shooting hoops with a bunch of other girls at the basketball courts.

"Trina's practicing with the Blue Jets," George whispered. "I knew I'd find her here."

"Ready, set?" Nancy whispered. "All systems go!"

The girls darted behind a tree with a thick trunk. From there they darted from tree to tree until they reached the one next to the court.

"Let's stick it to her!" Nancy said, holding up the glue bottle.

George held the basketball while Nancy squirted glue all over it.

"It's clear," Nancy pointed out. "So Trina won't have a clue it's glue."

"'Clue it's glue!'" Bess giggled. "You're a poet and you don't even know it—"

Thonk!

What was that? The girls looked down to see another basketball. It had hit the trunk and rolled around the tree.

"Somebody get my ball!" Trina's voice said.

"Throw Trina back the gluey one, George!" Nancy whispered.

George stepped out from behind the tree. She held up her gluey basketball and called, "Yo, Trina. Catch!"

George passed the ball to Trina. She caught it and said, "Thanks."

Nancy, Bess, and George stood by the tree to watch. Trina held up one hand to dribble the ball. But the ball was stuck to her hand!

"Hey! Hey!" Trina said. She pumped her hand up and down, trying to free the ball. "Did someone stick gum on this? I can't get it off! I can't get it off!"

"George, are you sure the site was Junior Sleuths?" Bess asked. "Or Junior Goofs?"

The girls were about to run when the ball finally dropped from Trina's hand with a *plunk*. Trina stared at the sticky web of glue dripping from her fingertips.

"What is this gross stuff?" Trina cried. "Some kind of alien ectoplasm?"

"No, Trina," Nancy called. "It's just glue. The same kind we use in arts and crafts."

Trina stared at the glue bottle in Nancy's hand.

"Why did you squirt glue on my basketball?" Trina demanded.

"It's not your ball, it's mine," George said. "Yours rolled behind the tree."

"We put glue on the ball to get your finger-prints," Bess explained.

"My fingerprints?" Trina exclaimed. She narrowed her eyes at the girls. "Does this have something to do with one of your cases?"

"Doesn't everything?" George asked.

"Somebody messed up our makeovers at Prissy's Princess Parlor yesterday," Nancy explained. "We thought you did it because you were mad at George."

"And," Bess added, "someone whose name we won't tell saw you coming out of Prissy's Princess Parlor yesterday."

"Are you guys nuts?" Trina cut in. "I'd rather kiss a pig on the lips than go into that prissy princess place!"

The Blue Jets mumbled in agreement.

"But somebody saw you!" Bess insisted.

Trina's face blushed red as she whisked Nancy, Bess, and George away from her team.

"Okay, okay, okay," Trina said with a low voice. "I was in that place yesterday, but only to buy blue face paint for our game. You know, blue for Blue Jets."

"Is that why your fingers are blue?" Nancy asked. "From smearing blue paint all over your face?"

"Yeah." Trina sighed. She stared at her fingers, still stained blue. "The stuff is hard to wash off."

"But if you weren't doing anything wrong, Trina," Bess said, "why did you rush out as if you didn't want someone to see you?"

"Because I *didn't* want anyone to see me!" Trina cried. "Everyone knows what I think of that place. If they found out I was there, they'd laugh me out of River Heights!"

"It's not that bad," George said. "The baseball-bat barrettes they gave me were pretty cool."

Trina leaned closer to the girls and whispered, "Just don't tell my team I was there. Pleeease?"

Before Nancy could answer Trina picked up her ball and ran back to her team.

"What do you think?" George asked.

"I think she had a good excuse," Bess said.

"What about the rest of her team?" Nancy said. "If they used the hard-to-get-out face paint, wouldn't they be blue too?"

"Watch this!" George said with a sly smile.

She ran onto the basketball court and shouted, "Blue Jets rock! High five!"

The girls on the team exchanged puzzled looks. Then they shrugged and high-fived George one by one.

Nancy didn't get it—until George ran back and said, "Three blue fingers, a blue chin, and two blue cheeks. They used the stuff too."

"Good work, George!" Nancy said, patting her on the shoulder. "Now we know Trina did go for the blue paint and not to mess up our makeovers."

"Trina Vanderhoof is clean!" Bess declared. Then added, ". . . after she washes that icky glue off her hand."

The girls walked back onto the court so George could pick up her gluey basketball.

"You guys," George told the Blue Jets, "if you rub baby oil all over those blue stains, you'll get them out."

"Really?" Trina asked.

"For sure," George said. "I once painted my

face orange for Halloween and the stuff came off like magic!"

"She went as a piece of candy corn," Bess said with a nod. "Next day you'd never have known it."

The Blue Jets smiled at George and thanked her. Trina was finally smiling too.

"Hey, we're playing the boys at school next week," Trina told George. "Want to play?"

"You bet!" George said. She looked down at her icky, sticky basketball. "But we'd better use *your* ball!"

Nancy, Bess, and George left the court and walked through the park. The sun was shining warm on the tops of their heads. Spring was definitely in the air—but as long as the case wasn't solved, so was trouble.

"Our only suspects are Suki and Ella," Nancy said. "Let's go back to our headquarters and see what we can dig up on them."

They passed the playground where Kevin Garcia was sitting on a swing. He wasn't swinging, just staring down at his sneakers.

"Let's show Kevin we're not scary anymore," Nancy suggested. She and her friends started walking toward the swing set.

"Hi, Kevin!" Nancy called.

Kevin looked up. When he saw the girls his mouth dropped open. Then he jumped off the swing and raced away.

"Kevin, wait!" Nancy called. What was up with him?

ChaPTER SEVEN

Knock, Knock, What's There?

"Does anyone have a mirror?" Bess asked as they watched Kevin charge out of the park gate.

"Why?" Nancy wanted to know.

"Maybe we still look scary!" Bess said. "Why else would Kevin look like a deer in head-lights?"

"We don't look scary anymore," Nancy insisted, although she had no idea why Kevin acted so weird either.

"Speaking of deer," George said as they left the park, "did Hannah ever find something stinky to keep deer away?"

"Not yet," Nancy replied.

"Too bad Hannah can't use the stinky stuff

that was in our hair yesterday," Bess said. "That would do the trick!"

Back at the Drew house Hannah fixed the girls tuna sandwiches for lunch. But after lunch it was back to work, as the girls headed straight up to Nancy's room.

George took her usual place at Nancy's computer. After opening up a case file she spun around and said, "Okay! What do we know about Suki and Ella so far?"

Nancy sat on her bed deep in thought. "They had a motive—a reason for wanting to do it," she said.

Bess was balancing on one foot, trying to copy the flamingo pose she had seen at Yay for Yoga.

"They could have sneaked the stinky blue stuff into the parlor yesterday," Bess said. "And poured it into the Strawberry Spritz bottle while we were in the back room."

"We were only in the back room for five minutes," Nancy pointed out.

"That's not enough time to do all that," George said. "First they had to unscrew the bottles, then pour—"

"I have an idea!" Nancy said, jumping up from the bed. "Let's be Rad Scientists just like Suki and Ella."

"Huh?" Bess asked.

"Let's do an experiment," Nancy explained. "We'll empty out a bottle, fill it with something else, and see how long it takes."

The girls ran downstairs to the kitchen. After rummaging through Hannah's recycling bin the girls found two empty bottles the same size as the Strawberry Spritz.

They carried the bottles upstairs to the bathroom and got to work. First Nancy filled both bottles with water and twisted on the caps. Next she placed them side-by-side on the sink counter.

Looking down at her watch George started the countdown: "Five . . . four . . . three . . . two . . . one . . . go!"

Quickly Nancy untwisted the cap of one

bottle. She poured the water into the sink and down the drain. Next she untwisted the other bottle cap.

"Go, Nancy, go!" Bess cheered.

Nancy poured water from the full bottle into the empty one. After tossing away the empty bottle she twisted the cap on the newly filled one and shouted, "Done!"

"Two minutes and forty-five seconds!" George said, tapping her watch.

"Plenty of time for Suki and Ella to do the switcheroo," Bess declared. "They're guilty as charged."

"Not yet," Nancy reminded her friends. "First we have to ask them some questions."

"No," George said. "First we have to *find* them!"

Luckily for the Clue Crew, the Rad Scientists had their own website. It listed the address of their clubhouse, and their next meeting, Friday morning at ten o'clock.

"Tomorrow is Friday," Nancy said, folding her arms across her chest. "That's when we'll find out if those Rad Scientists are *bad* scientists!"

"Are you sure Suki and Ella messed up your makeovers, Nancy?" Mr. Drew asked that night while preparing dinner.

"Pretty sure, Daddy," Nancy said, trying to stop Chip from begging at the counter. "Suki and Ella had a reason to do it on purpose."

"Unless," he said. "It was a mistake."

"Why would Suki and Ella make a mistake?" Nancy asked.

"Unless it wasn't Suki and Ella," Mr. Drew said with a little wink.

"Daddy!" Nancy sighed.

Her father was great at helping with her cases. But today he was making her head spin!

Chip's ears suddenly perked up as the door-bell rang.

"I'll see who it is," Nancy said. "You're busy making dinner."

"Busy making a mess!" Mr. Drew groaned as he spilled cut vegetables onto the floor.

Nancy ran out of the kitchen and down the hall. She stood on her toes and peeked through the tiny window on the front door. There was no one outside.

Unless it's a short kid, Nancy thought.

Opening the door a crack, Nancy peeked outside. Still no one there. About to shut the door,

Nancy spotted something on the doorstep. It was a brown-wrapped package with her name written across it.

Nancy stared down at the package. Who was it from? What was inside?

"Daddy!" Nancy shouted over her shoulder. "I just got some weird package!"

ChaPTER EiGhT

Hide and Sneak

Nancy watched as her father ripped off the brown paper. Underneath was a box with the words "Munchy Crunchy" printed on it.

"Candy bars?" Nancy asked.

"Granola bars," Mr. Drew said as he opened the box.

"Yummy!" Nancy exclaimed. Inside were a dozen granola bars, some with fruit, nuts—even chocolate chips!

"We know what's inside," Mr. Drew said, rummaging through the box. "But there's no note or return address."

"I don't have a clue who sent them to me," Nancy said, shaking her head.

"Then don't eat them until you know for sure," Mr. Drew suggested. "I'll put the box in the kitchen for now."

Mr. Drew carried the mysterious box into the house. Chip picked up the brown paper between her teeth and swung it back and forth.

"A secret package," Nancy said. She sighed as she tugged the paper out of her puppy's mouth. "Things are getting nuttier than those granola bars!"

But the next morning when Nancy met Bess and George, things got even stranger.

"You got granola bars too?" Nancy gasped.

"A whole box," Bess said.

"Some of my granola bars had butterscotch chips!" George said, pulling a wrapped bar from her pocket. "My mom told me not to eat any until I know who gave them to me."

"That's what Daddy told me," Nancy said. "I wonder if those granola bars have something to do with our case."

"Who knows?" George said as she dropped the bar back into her pocket. "But as soon as we find out who sent them—snack attack!"

The girls made their way toward the Rad Scientists clubhouse. A red mailbox outside read, SUSSMAN FAMILY.

"But where's the clubhouse?" Nancy wondered.

Carefully and quietly, the girls scouted the Sussman yard. The garage door was open and the girls peeked inside.

There was no car, just two bicycles, folded lawn chairs, and a green Hula-hoop resting against the wall. But then Nancy spotted something else—a long table covered with a white tablecloth. On the table were clear test tubes and beakers—the kind they used in science class. There was also a lump of clay molded into the shape of a mountain.

"It's a mad scientist's lab!" Bess gasped.

"More like a Rad Scientist's lab," Nancy pointed out. "I think we just found their clubhouse."

"Come on," George said, stepping into the

garage. "Let's go inside and look for clues."

"What if the Rad Scientists show up?" Nancy asked.

"Or Dr. Frankenstein?" Bess said with a shudder. "He might be a member too!"

"Don't wimp out now, you guys," George said as she walked toward the table. "There might be traces of stinky blue stuff in those glass tubes."

Nancy knew George was right. She darted into the garage. Bess followed, calling, "Wait for meeeeee!"

George was examining the test tubes when Nancy and Bess reached the table. "No blue stuff anywhere," she said.

Nancy took a whiff of a beaker filled with clear liquid. She wrinkled her nose and said, "Ugh. Vinegar!"

"Vinegar?" George repeated. "What are they making in here—salad dressing?"

Bess pointed to the clay mountain. Circling the base were tiny stalks of broccoli arranged to look like trees.

"They're making an erupting volcano, you guys," Bess said. "Vinegar mixed with baking soda will make it gush."

"How do you know?" George asked.

"I helped my neighbor Bradley Buchalter build one for the science fair," Bess explained. "It won first prize."

Bess grabbed a box of baking soda. Nancy gasped as she poured some into the mouth of the volcano.

"Don't touch anything, Bess!" Nancy cried.

The moment Bess stopped, Nancy saw three figures heading toward the garage. It was Suki,

Ella, and a younger boy. They were too busy talking to notice the girls but Nancy's stomach did a triple-flip anyway.

"Hide!" Nancy whispered.

In a blink the Clue Crew ducked under the tablecloth. Huddled beneath the table, they could hear Suki, Ella, and the boy enter the garage.

"Okay, Ernest," Ella's voice said. "If you want to join Rad Scientists, you have to pass our test."

"Think you can make that volcano over there erupt?" Suki's voice asked.

"Are you kidding?" Ernest laughed. "I've been exploding volcanoes since kindergarten. Bring it on!"

Nancy held her breath as three pairs of sneakers appeared beneath the tablecloth. Suki, Ella, and Ernest were standing right next to them!

"First you take three tablespoons of baking soda," Ernest's voice explained. "And pour it into the volcano."

"See?" Bess whispered.

"Shh!" Nancy whispered back.

"Next take a half-cup of vinegar," Ernest went on. "Pour it inside and—"

Whoooooosh!!

"Holy cannoli!" Ernest cried. "I created Mount Vesuvius!"

Nancy, Bess, and George shrieked. A thick fizzy liquid was oozing over the side of the table!

"Hey!" Suki shouted as the girls scrambled out of hiding. "What are you doing here?"

Nancy straightened up and gulped. Now the Rad Scientists were definitely *mad* scientists!

ChaPTeR NiNe

Natural Disaster

"I don't know what happened," Ernest admitted. "I added the right amount of vinegar and baking soda."

"Um . . . we were kind of playing with the volcano before you came," Bess muttered. "I mean . . . I was."

"So if it wasn't my fault, can I still join the club?" Ernest asked excitedly.

"Forget the volcano," Suki said. "Right now I want to know what the Clue Crew is doing in my garage."

"Spying on us?" Ella asked, raising an eyebrow.

"I guess you could say that," George said.

"Someone messed with our makeovers at Prissy's Princess Parlor the other day."

"And you were there!" Bess declared.

"Princess? Makeovers?" Ernest cried. "If that's what this club is about—I'm outta here!"

Ernest's wet sneakers squeaked as he stomped out of the garage.

"Who needs him anyway?" Suki grumbled. "His science fair project was an ant farm. Big deal."

"Don't change the subject," Nancy warned. "Did you or didn't you mess with our makeovers?"

"We didn't!" Ella insisted.

"We were mad, but we got over it," Suki said. "Especially after we got these awesome manicures."

Suki and Ella lifted their hands to reveal perfectly polished nails in colors of the rainbow!

"Nancy . . . George," Bess whispered as she waved them to the side. "I think they're telling the truth!"

"How do you know?" Nancy whispered.

"Their nails were wet when they left the Princess Parlor," Bess explained. "If they did all that unscrewing and pouring, their manicures would have been a mess."

"You're right," Nancy gasped.

"Leave it to a girly-girl to figure that one out," George said with a grin.

Nancy, Bess, and George walked back to the Rad Scientists, this time with smiles on their faces.

"We know you didn't do it," Nancy admitted. "Sorry we were snooping around in here."

The girls were about to leave when Suki said, "Sorry we acted so creepy about the contest. We know you didn't jump the line."

"We just wanted to win so badly," Ella sighed.

"And while we're apologizing," Bess said. "I'm sorry for messing with your volcano. I just wanted to show Nancy and George how it erupts."

"Did you ever build an erupting volcano?" Ella asked.

"I helped Bradley Buchalter build his," Bess explained. "I really like to build things and—"

"Bradley Buchalter?" Suki squealed. "He's a science rock star!"

"Can you get Bradley to join Rad Scientists?" Ella begged Bess. "Pretty please—with $C_{12}H_{22}O_{11}$ on top?"

"What's that?" Bess asked.

"The chemical formula for sugar," Ella explained.

"Oh, and you guys can join our club too," Suki added. "You already passed the volcano test."

Nancy couldn't believe it. They had gone

from enemies to friends in just minutes!

"Thanks, but no thanks," Nancy said. "We're too busy solving our mysteries."

"But when we need help with our science homework," George said, giving a thumbs-up, "we're here!"

Nancy, Bess, and George were glad they made two new friends. But they were not glad they had run out of suspects.

"We can't give up," Nancy said, back at their headquarters. "So stop groaning, George."

"That's not me!" George said, spinning around in the chair. "It's my stomach growling because I need a snack."

George pulled out her granola bar. She was about to unwrap it when Nancy cut in.

"Don't, George," Nancy warned.

"It's probably safe," George said. She pointed to the wrapper. "It's all natural and from the Mean Bean."

"That Strawberry Spritz was all natural too,"

Bess said. "And look what it did to us."

Mean Bean? All natural? The words hit Nancy like a ton of butterscotch chips. She ran to her jacket lying on the bed. Reaching into the pocket she pulled out the label with the blue smudge.

Nancy read the label under the blue stain. The bottle of Strawberry Spritz was from the Mean Bean too!

"Mean Bean . . . Kevin Garcia!" Nancy figured out loud. "Maybe the granola bars came from him."

"Anybody can buy stuff at the Mean Bean," George said.

"But Kevin has been acting weird lately, remember?" Nancy said. "So if the Strawberry Spritz came from his parents' store, maybe he knows something we don't!"

ChAPTER TEN

Princess Power!

The first place the Clue Crew looked for Kevin was in the Mean Bean Health Store.

"This place always smells like vitamins," George whispered as they walked in. Mrs. Garcia was behind the counter ringing up a customer. Mr. Garcia's back was to the girls as he counted boxes of oatmeal on a shelf.

"I don't see Kevin," Nancy said. "But while we're here there's something I want to check out."

Nancy led her friends to the shelf marked "Natural Beauty Products." She smiled at a whole shelf filled with Strawberry Spritz.

"Kevin could have gotten a bottle easily," Nancy pointed out.

"And there's a ton of granola bars!" George said, nodding toward a shelf filled with health snacks. "Just like the kind we got."

"Shh," Bess whispered. "There's Kevin."

Nancy turned to see Kevin. He was holding a shovel as he slipped out the back door.

"Where's he going with that?" George asked.

"There's only one way to find out," Nancy said.

The girls scurried to the back. Nancy opened the door and they peeked outside. Kevin was using the shovel to dig in the backyard.

"Ahoy, Captain Garcia," George called, swinging the door wide open. "Digging for buried treasure?"

Kevin paled as the girls approached.

"No," he said as he kept shoveling. "I'm planting seeds for the spring. I'll bet you didn't know we had an herb garden back here."

Nancy looked into the hole. Sticking out from underneath some dirt was a green plastic thermos bottle.

"What's in the bottle?" Nancy asked. She was about to reach down for it when Kevin snatched it up.

"Get that bottle!" Bess shouted as Kevin ran to the back fence.

George chased Kevin to the fence. As he began climbing she grabbed hold of his sneaker.

"Whoa!" Kevin shouted as he lost his grip.

He tumbled to the ground and the cap popped off the bottle. Gushing out all over Kevin was a blue liquid—and it smelled like rotten eggs!

"Ew!" Bess said, squeezing her nose.

"That's the stuff that was in our hair!" Nancy said, trying hard not to breathe. "I'd know it anywhere."

Kevin dropped the bottle as he stood up. "Oh, well," he muttered. "At least I won't be chased by deer."

"Deer?" George asked. "Why deer?"

Kevin nodded down at his blue-stained shirt. "This stuff was a natural deer repellent I invented," he said.

Nancy stared at Kevin and said, "You mean like what Hannah wanted?"

Kevin nodded.

"I felt bad that the Mean Bean didn't have what you needed," Kevin said. "So I researched the stuff that deer hated to smell."

"What do they hate to smell?" Bess asked.

"Mostly rotten eggs," Kevin said. "So I mixed up some eggs, garlic, onion, and green food dye that would blend in with the plants and bushes."

"But the stuff was blue," George said.

"I didn't have any yellow to make green so I just used blue instead," Kevin said. "Close enough."

"Then what happened?" Nancy urged.

"I needed a spray bottle so I emptied out some Strawberry Spritz," Kevin explained. "I poured my brew into the empty bottle then put it back on the shelf so the eggs would get nice and rotten."

"It did the trick," George muttered.

"I put my bottle apart from the others so I'd know which one it was," Kevin went on. "But when I went to get it the next morning, it was gone."

"What happened to it?" Nancy asked.

"My parents said they took some bottles to Prissy's Princess Parlor," Kevin said, his shoulders sagging. "I knew they took the one with my deer repellent too!"

"Why didn't you tell someone?" Nancy asked.

"I ran to the parlor to stop those ladies from using it," Kevin admitted. "But by the time I got there—"

"We were already blue-headed monsters." Bess sighed.

"Sorry." Kevin sighed. He pointed to the bottle on the ground. "The stuff was too stinky to pour down the drain so I tried burying it instead."

"Did you also leave us a bunch of granola bars without signing your name?" Nancy asked.

"It was a peace offering," Kevin said. He heaved a big sigh. "But I wouldn't blame you if you hated me forever."

Nancy felt bad for Kevin. He didn't mean to mess up their makeovers. He just wanted to help by inventing a deer repellent.

"We don't hate you, Kevin." Nancy said.

"Just the way you smell right now," Bess said, scrunching up her nose.

"But you really should explain everything to Prissy and Wendy," Nancy said, "so they can reopen their store."

Kevin held up his blue-stained arms and said, "Can I go take a shower first?"

"You'd better take about ten!" George groaned.

The girls said good-bye to Kevin. Then they left the Mean Bean, smiling all the way. Another case solved by the Clue Crew!

It wasn't long before Prissy's Princess Parlor was open for business again. That Sunday Nancy, Bess, and George were invited back for brand-new makeovers!

This time Nancy and Bess were treated to cool hairstyles, pearly-pink lip gloss and princess-perfect manicures. George was happy to have new baseball-bat barrettes back in her hair and silver nails that matched her sneaker laces. Instead of rotten eggs the girls smelled like strawberries, thanks to the *real* Strawberry Spritz!

"Say cheese!" the photographer said as Nancy, Bess, and George posed in front of the castle-gate door.

"Will we be on the front page?" Bess asked.

The reporter stepped forward with that day's edition of the River Heights *Daily News.*

"Not today!" she replied, holding up the paper. Nancy's eyes widened when she saw Kevin on the front page. The headline read: KID GENIUS MAKES DEER STEER CLEAR!

"It's Kevin and his deer repellent!" Nancy exclaimed.

"Now you can buy some for Hannah," Bess said happily.

"And Kevin can join the Rad Scientists," George added.

The reporter put down the paper and picked up her pad. "So, girls," she said, getting ready to write. "How does it feel to be princesses?"

Nancy traded smiles with Bess and George. She knew that her best friends were thinking the same thing she was.

"Being princesses for a day is cool," Nancy declared. "But we'd rather be detectives *every* day!"

Dress Up Your 'Do!

Bad hair day? Never again, when you wear a stunning new headband you decorate yourself. Just follow these easy tips for turning a plain headband from boring to beautiful!

What You'll Need:
Plain plastic headband
Long strand of colored ribbon
Craft glue

Ready, Set . . . Wrap!

❋ Carefully glue one end of the ribbon to one end of the headband; wait for glue to dry.

❋ Begin wrapping the ribbon tightly around the headband (dot some glue along the headband for extra hold).

❋ Once the whole headband is covered, glue the other end of the ribbon to the opposite end of the headband.

✤ Using craft scissors, snip off the leftover ribbon.

That's a Wrap,
But the Fun Isn't Done

Go color-crazy by wrapping more ribbons of different hues. For serious zing, add some bling, such as jewel-like crystals glued to the ribbon. String colorful beads on the ribbon as you wrap—or sew on buttons or bows. You can even decorate barrettes and hair clips the same way!

See? You don't need a princess parlor to get a smart, dazzling 'do. All you need is imagination, a bit of glue, and most important—YOU!

Join the CLUE CREW
& solve these other cases!